C.S. JAMES

TOY HORROR STORY

Welcome back!

I didn't expect to see you again so soon. I was certain I had frightened you away.

. . .what's that? You want something *scarier*? I think I have just the story to do the trick!

Don't worry. This story ends with a smile.

I just won't say whose.

Are you ready to be **SHOOK**?

C.S. James

ONE

Brogan Fernsby loved to play practical jokes.

Even as a toddler learning how to walk, he would purposely fall over in front of his parents, Mr. and Mrs. Fernsby, and pretend to cry that he was hurt. When one of them would run over to make sure he was okay, Brogan would tilt his head back, laugh till he snorted, and crawl away smiling.

His parents didn't find it very funny.

While Brogan continued to find the hilarity in the many pranks he pulled, the victims of his shenanigans didn't always feel the same way.

In fact, they never did.

But Brogan didn't care. He kept growing and joking, and as he got older, his pranks became more thought out. More sophisticated.

Then, last April, Brogan pulled off the greatest prank of all time — according to Brogan, anyway. It was so epic that his friend, Gabriel, recorded it and posted it to YouTube for the whole world to see. And the video got over a million hits!

Brogan felt like a celebrity the entire month. Everyone in his class thought he was the coolest kid at school. People recognized him while he was out shopping with his mom. Even his little sister's lame friends wanted to come over to the house just to see him.

He felt on top of the world!

But those fifteen minutes of fame couldn't last, and didn't.

In September, his dad called for a family meeting.

"I got a new job," Mr. Fernsby revealed. "It's in Indiana. We'll be moving next month."

And now here the four of them were, crammed into Mr. Fernsby's blue Honda, driving across three states to get to their new house.

"Are we there yet?" Cammie asked from her booster seat, her hundredth time doing so. Brogan's little sister was only five and didn't have a patient bone in her body.

"Are you going to ask that every two minutes?" Brogan sighed.

"We're almost there," Mr. Fernsby assured them from the driver's seat.

"Good, because Isabella is getting super impatient!" Cammie said.

Isabella was Cammie's vintage doll. She was about two and a half feet tall, made of plastic, and wore a tattered black dress. Her face was pale and soft, and her lips were painted into a slight smile. If you squinted hard enough, she somewhat resembled the Mona Lisa.

Brogan hated Isabella. Not only was her face super creepy, but she had a weird smell that just wouldn't seem to go away. And because Cammie insisted on taking her everywhere she went, Brogan always had to put up with her eerie face and insufferable smell as long as he was in her presence.

Brogan sighed again. "Why can't Isabella be in the back and Coco stay up here with us?"

Coco was the family's small Boston Terrier. The dog whined from her kennel in the vehicle's cargo area. Her tiny paws tapped the plastic floor.

"You know long car rides bother Coco," Mr. Fernsby replied. "Besides, remember when Coco tried to tear Isabella apart?"

"Can you blame her?" Brogan muttered.

"She stays in her kennel," Mr. Fernsby stated.

Brogan looked back sympathetically at the dog, then settled back into his seat.

"This is a beautiful town," Mrs. Fernsby noted, glancing out the window at the passing scenery.

"Sure is," Mr. Fernsby agreed. "This is going to be a good change for us. I can feel it."

Brogan didn't care how beautiful the town was, or what it had to offer him that his old place didn't.

It just wasn't home.

Brogan sat silently in the backseat, rolling his Canon video camera back and forth in his hands. It was a gift from his parents after his YouTube video blew up — a gesture on their part to encourage Brogan to "vlog" with the camera and document his daily life.

Little did his parents know he would mostly use it against them to play more pranks.

None of his other prank videos ever came close to matching the success of his first one, but Brogan didn't let that stop him from trying to repeat it.

Over and over and over again.

The family's blue Honda pulled off the main road, entering a quiet neighborhood full of massive two-story homes and sugar maple trees.

"Is this where we live?" Cammie asked as she leaned closer to her window. She propped Isabella up to take a peek.

"This is our neighborhood," Mr. Fernsby replied.

"These trees are gorgeous," Mrs. Fernsby said. "I love the way they change colors around this time of year."

"Which house is ours?" Brogan asked, leaning over in his seat to stare out the windshield.

"Last house on the left," Mr. Fernsby said and pointed.

The Honda slowed as it reached the cul-de-sac at the end of the road. Mr. Fernsby turned the wheel to the left, pulling the vehicle into the driveway. "Home sweet home," he said.

The dark, Victorian house stood at the end of the driveway, and collectively, the family sat in silence and admired it.

The first thing Brogan noticed about the house was the sheer size of it. It was at least three times as big as his last house. Like other homes in the neighborhood, it was two stories tall, full of windows, and even had multiple chimneys jutting out of the roof. There was a wraparound porch on the left, and part of the house even appeared to extend over the driveway, almost like the hotel the family had stayed at when they went to Disney World.

"It's huge!" Cammie suddenly shouted, breaking the silence. "I get to pick my room first!"

"Over my dead body!" Brogan replied, and they both unclicked their seatbelts at the same time.

As Cammie opened her door, grabbed Isabella, and shuffled out to freedom, Mr. Fernsby reached back to stop Brogan.

"Wait a minute," Mr. Fernsby said to him. "Don't forget about Coco. She needs to use the bathroom first."

"But Dad!" Brogan huffed. "Cammie's going to pick the best room!" Then he watched in frustration as Cammie enthusiastically traipsed up the driveway, doll in tow.

"May I remind you that *you* wanted a dog, Brogan," Mr. Fernsby said. And that was true. Brogan was the one who begged his parents for a dog for over a year, even though Cammie was the reason he got stuck with Coco. Brogan really wanted the Great Dane the animal shelter had named Walter, but big dogs scared Cammie, so the family decided on Coco instead.

Brogan looked back at the dog's kennel and stared at Coco with a perfect mix of resentment and pity. He loved the dog, but he hated that he did.

"Besides," Mrs. Fernsby chimed in, "the house is huge, Brogan. All the bedrooms are amazing. You'll see."

Unconvinced, Brogan said nothing, grabbed Coco's leash from the floor, and opened his door.

Mr. Fernsby popped the hatch for Brogan, who made his way to the rear of the vehicle. As the hatchback door rose with a hydraulic whisper, Brogan reached in and opened the door to Coco's kennel.

The dog bolted.

"*Coco!*" Brogan shrieked. The dog hit the ground and took off as fast as her legs would carry her. His parents facepalmed as Brogan grunted in aggravation.

"Go get her!" Mrs. Fernsby exclaimed.

Brogan let out an annoyed scream and hurriedly gave chase. "Coco, *stop!*"

But the dog didn't stop. A moving furball of curiosity and excitement, Coco bounded down the middle of the road, leaving the cul-de-sac and coming to the neighborhood's first four-way intersection.

Brogan advanced on the dog, and as he did, his thoughts clouded with an image of Cammie picking the best room in the house and rubbing it in his face. He could practically hear her teasing voice in his ears as she flaunted her superiority. His eyes narrowed. He was more annoyed than ever.

I hate this family, he thought.

Then Brogan heard a sound that snapped him back to reality. A low, mechanical humming rising in the distance.

Brogan recognized the sound immediately, and his eyes blossomed in their sockets until he was staring wide-eyed at the intersection, silently hoping he was wrong.

But he wasn't.

In the distance, a large yellow moving truck bounded up the road — heading straight for Coco.

TWO

The color left Brogan's face. His heart sank to his feet. Suddenly the mental image of his sister picking a room before he could felt trivial next to the one of his dog lying flattened and dead in the middle of the road.

"*Coco!*" he shouted over the roar of the approaching truck.

But there was nothing he could do. Helpless and afraid to look, Brogan closed his eyes.

Miraculously, the dog stopped in her tracks, sniffed at the air, then pranced to the safety of the roadside where some bulk garbage had been placed on the curb.

The truck barreled by.

Brogan peeked between his fingers, then let out a sigh of relief when he saw Coco alive and unharmed.

Whew, he thought. That was too close!

In the distance, the truck advanced to the cul-de-sac and parked against the curb of his new house.

Coco trotted into the grass and did her business, then happily came to Brogan with her tail wagging.

"You're a real pain in the butt," he said to her.

Coco yipped and panted in response.

"Come on. Let's go see the new house."

Brogan picked up the dog and headed back. When he got to the house, he saw his parents having a heated discussion with the movers. Something about a glass coffee table being cracked. His mother looked angry about it.

Brogan continued past them and put Coco in the fenced-in backyard. She stuck close to the fencing, keeping her nose to the ground and sniffing the perimeter. Brogan watched her for a moment, then locked the gate and returned to the front of the house.

Time to pick a bedroom, Brogan thought.

Yeah, right. Time to find out what I'm getting stuck with is more like it.

Brogan entered the house through the front door. The hinges creaked and echoed through the empty foyer.

Brogan looked around. There was a living room to the left, an office to the right, and a large bifurcated staircase straight head. The walls were painted a dark blue, and all the doors and trim were stained with a deep Kona finish. He thought it was strange that such a big house with so many windows could be so dark inside.

A sound echoed from upstairs. Brogan looked up. He could hear the pitter-patter of Cammie's footsteps as she explored the second floor. He reluctantly made his way up the steps to join her.

When he got to the top of the landing, he stopped and looked left and right, unsure of which way to go. Finally, he committed to a direction and went right. It ultimately didn't matter which way he went — the entire upstairs seemed to overlook and circle around the foyer, anyway.

Brogan approached the first open door and stuck his head into the room.

"*BOO!*"

Brogan flinched as a figure jumped out at him.

"Stop it, Cammie!" he screamed.

"Ha! Ha! I scared you!" his little sister laughed.

"You did not," he protested. Even though Cammie *did* surprise him, he'd never admit it to her. He didn't want to inflate her sense of self-worth even more, if that was even possible.

"This is my room," Cammie revealed. She proudly gestured with her hands, showcasing the room like it was the grand prize to be won on a TV game show.

Brogan looked around. The room was breathtaking. It had tall ceilings, a door leading out to a private balcony, and an iron chandelier. It looked like something you'd see in a medieval castle.

"This room's okay," Brogan lied, again not wanting to feed her self-pride. But in the pit of his stomach, a seed of jealousy had already started to take root.

"It's the biggest room — besides Mom and Dad's," Cammie said. "And look at this!"

Cammie proceeded to the corner of the room where a small tray had been screwed into the drywall. She grabbed a red piece of chalk from it and started drawing on the wall.

"What are you *doing*!?" Brogan exclaimed and moved in to stop her.

"It's chalk paint!" Cammie replied. Then she wiped the drawing away with her sleeve and clapped her hands together to get the chalk dust off. "It's the only room that has it. Cool, huh?"

"Whatever," Brogan replied and turned to walk away.

A host of obscenities he wouldn't dream of saying out loud flooded his thoughts as he stomped out of the room. Of *course* Cammie would pick the biggest room in the house with a private balcony and cool chandelier and walls you could draw on. And of *course* she would rub it in his face and let him know what he was missing out on.

He hoped the other bedrooms might offer something he could rub in *her* face, but when he saw the two remaining rooms, he sighed with disappointment. They were both pretty plain. Sure, the ceilings were just as tall and the rooms were decently sized, but he didn't see a private balcony or medieval chandelier in either of them, and he certainly couldn't draw on the walls (unless he wanted it to stay there permanently and risk getting scolded by his parents).

There just wasn't anything special about either room.

Brogan kicked the baseboard in frustration.

I *really* hate this family, he thought for the second time in under an hour.

With no other factors to persuade him, he ultimately made his decision based on the color of the room. One room was dark blue, like the walls in the foyer downstairs; the other was a forest green.

"Green it is," he said to himself, feeling a little green with envy himself.

Brogan walked to his bedroom window and looked out. His view overlooked the front yard, and he could see two movers struggling to carry a couch up the driveway.

At least I'll be able to see when the bus gets here for school, he thought.

Brogan stepped back from the window. His footsteps echoed in the empty room.

It won't echo so much when my stuff is in here, he assured himself.

Brogan started to picture what the room would look like with all his things, and he started mapping out where he would put his bed, dresser, desk, and TV.

He thought about putting his bed near the window, but then he realized the length of it would probably prevent the closet door from opening all the way.

Wait, the closet! Brogan realized he hadn't even seen what his closet looked like.

His disappointment with the room slowly turned to excitement as he wondered how big his closet was. Maybe it would be bigger than Cammie's and he could brag about it later at dinner.

It'd be a small victory, but a victory, nonetheless.

Brogan advanced to the closet.

Strange. It was bolt-latched at the top. He'd never seen that on a closet door before.

Brogan had to jump to slide the latch all the way over. It took two tries, but he finally was able to unlock it and open the door.

"Ohh!" Brogan jumped back and gasped.

Inside, a grinning face stared back at him.

THREE

Brogan did a double take, then quickly turned on the closet light to get a better look.

There was a clown doll sitting on the shelf.

Three feet tall and rail thin, the clown wore a purple ringmaster suit, white gloves, and black shoes. Orange hair sprouted from the sides of his head in sharp triangular points, almost in the shape of shark fins. The top of his head was bald, and it sort of looked like he used to wear a hat that was mistakenly ripped off.

But it was the clown's smile Brogan noticed most of all. It was wide and toothy, curving unnaturally upwards in a grin unlike any Brogan had ever seen before.

Brogan reached out and lifted the doll from the shelf. It was lightweight and seemed to be made of some type of plastic and stuffing.

Brogan flicked the clown's bowtie with his thumb and index finger, then glanced down at the clown's shoe. He squeezed it.

The shoe squeaked.

Brogan smiled and squeezed it again, then again, and soon he was rapidly squeezing the shoe as if it were the bulb of a blood pressure cuff. It amused him, to say the least.

Brogan looked at the underside of the clown's shoe where something had been handwritten in permanent marker.

"*Mr. Squeaks*," Brogan read aloud. Then he squeezed the shoe a final time for good measure. "I guess that name makes sense. Nice to meet you, Mr. Squeaks."

Brogan carried the clown to the window, seeing both their reflections in the glass. He noticed how the clown's orange hair seemed to match the color of his own.

A light bulb suddenly turned on in his head, and his smile widened.

It was the same smile he had whenever he came up with a new idea for a prank.

Brogan set Mr. Squeaks on the floor and opened his bedroom window. He stuck his head out, then waved down to his dad, who was carrying a lamp up the driveway.

"Hey, Dad!" Brogan called out, waving.

Mr. Fernsby waved back and continued walking.

"Check this out!"

"Brogan, I'm busy. . ."

"Just watch!"

Brogan disappeared from his father's view. He grabbed Mr. Squeaks from the floor and then, making sure to keep his own body hidden below the sill, carefully lifted the doll up to the window.

Keeping hold of the doll's hand, Brogan tossed Mr. Squeaks out the window.

Down below, Mr. Fernsby watched in horror as a small human figure with orange hair — a faint doppelgänger of his own son — flew through the open window and then dangled from the ledge.

"Brogan, what are you DOING!?" Mr. Fernsby screamed, and he dropped the lamp with a deafening clank and sprinted to the front door.

20

Brogan pulled the doll back inside and fell onto his back in hysterics.

Seconds later, Mr. Fernsby exploded into the bedroom. Exhausted and out of breath, he looked curiously at Brogan, who was still laughing his head off, then at the strange-looking clown doll on the floor.

"What. . .how. . ." was all Mr. Fernsby could manage to get out as Brogan collected himself, grabbed Mr. Squeaks, and stood up.

"It's a clown doll," Brogan explained, still chuckling. "I just found him."

His father, unamused, could only stare.

"Did you really think it was *me* hanging out the window?" Brogan asked with a sly smile. "Come on, Dad, I don't have a bald spot!"

It took Mr. Fernsby a moment to compose himself. "That wasn't funny," he finally told his son. "That wasn't funny at all."

Mrs. Fernsby walked into the room, concern on her face. "What's going on?"

"I'm gonna kill that kid — that's what's going on!" Mr. Fernsby threw his hands in the air, stormed past his wife, and left the room.

Mrs. Fernsby looked at Brogan questionably. "What did you do now?" she asked. "And where'd you get *that*?" She gestured to Mr. Squeaks.

"In the closet," Brogan said. "The people who lived here before us must've left him. His name is Mr. Squeaks. I can keep him, right?"

Mrs. Fernsby looked at Brogan for a moment, her expression a mix of reasoning and reluctance.

"Yeah. OK, fine," Mrs. Fernsby breathed. "But no more jokes, Brogan. This move is stressful enough as it is. Deal?"

"Deal," Brogan agreed.

Mrs. Fernsby smiled at him, hesitant to believe him but having no other choice in the matter. She turned around and quietly walked out.

Alone again with his new discovery, Brogan turned Mr. Squeaks around and looked into the clown's wide, expressive eyes.

"You and me are going to have some fun," Brogan said.

Little did he know how wrong he was.

FOUR

"It's not fair!" Cammie pouted and kicked her legs under the table.

It was the end of a long day, and the family was finally eating dinner — takeout Chinese food. Everyone ate with chopsticks, except for Cammie, who hadn't mastered the skill.

"Cammie, settle down," Mr. Fernsby said, his voice soft but direct.

"Why didn't *my* room have anything in it!?" Cammie asked. She had been complaining all day about Brogan finding Mr. Squeaks in his closet.

"You picked your room first," Brogan muttered under his breath. Then he snuck a piece of beef to Coco, who was sitting patiently next to his chair.

"Your brother's right, Cammie," Mr. Fernsby agreed. "Your room has some things in it that he didn't have in his. I'd say Mr. Squeaks is a fair tradeoff. Even if he did try to give me a heart attack with it."

Brogan stuck out his tongue at his sister, and Cammie's face soured in response.

"Maybe you can compromise," Mrs. Fernsby interjected, playing mediator.

Brogan's tongue retreated into his mouth faster than measuring tape rolling back into its home. "Compromise?"

"Why don't you both alternate weeks with the doll?" Mrs. Fernsby suggested.

Brogan could already feel his face getting hot. "*No way!*" he contended.

A smile slowly crept across Cammie's face.

"It's simple," Mrs. Fernsby continued. "You take Mr. Squeaks this week, and Cammie can have him the next week, and so on." She took a bite of orange chicken.

"Oh *come on*, Mom!" Brogan huffed. "Cammie already has her stupid Isabella doll!"

"There's no reason why both of you can't play with it," Mrs. Fernsby replied.

"Sharing is caring," Cammie chimed in. "That's what my teacher told me." Then she stuck *her* tongue out at him.

"I already share my existence with you!" Brogan shouted. "That should be enough, you mutant!"

"*Brogan!*" Mr. and Mrs. Fernsby said together and dropped their chopsticks. They stared daggers at him.

Outnumbered and defeated, Brogan huffed, kicked his chair out, and crossed his arms. He didn't eat another bite.

✻   ✻   ✻

Brogan was still in a foul mood by the time he went to bed. He couldn't believe Cammie was getting her way *yet again*. And why? She already had her own doll. She got first choice for the bedroom she wanted. She basically even picked the family dog. Why did she always want what *he* had? Why did she have to make everything about her?

As he changed into his pajamas, Brogan looked around his room. He hadn't been able to unpack his personal things earlier in the day, so he couldn't help feeling like his own room didn't even belong to him. Like it would somehow get swiped out from under his nose at any moment.

Honestly, was there anything that *only* belonged to him?

Brogan looked across the room and saw his video camera sitting on the dresser. He picked it up and clicked it on, looking through the viewfinder as he swept the camera from side to side.

At least Cammie can't have *this*, he thought to himself.

Brogan remembered when Cammie first made a big fuss about the camera. She begged and pleaded for a turn with it, but he and his parents knew she would probably break it. Cammie was very clumsy, after all. It was the only time he could remember all of them being equally against the idea and telling her no.

Aside from his fifteen minutes of internet fame, watching Cammie break down after not getting her way was one of the best moments of his life.

He wished he could see it again.

Still holding the camera, Brogan aimed the viewfinder at Mr. Squeaks. He was sitting on the nightstand, legs and arms hanging limp and twisted. The clown's head was cocked to the side, but his eyes were focused directly on Brogan.

A little creeped out, Brogan took a step to the left, then to the right. It was eerie the way the clown's eyes seemed to follow him no matter which way he went. Like one of those spooky portraits you'd see on the wall of a haunted house.

Mr. Squeaks really *was* kind of creepy.

Then, Brogan smiled.

A big smile.

That "new idea" smile.

Except this time, his smile was so big that his round cheeks nearly covered his eyes.

It was at that moment he knew *exactly* how he was going to get back at Cammie.

There was a knock on the door.

"Lights out, Brogan!" his father called from the hallway.

"Doing it now," Brogan replied as he placed the camcorder in the bottom drawer of his dresser. Then he crawled under the covers.

"Goodnight," Mr. Fernsby said through the wooden barrier.

"Goodnight, Dad," Brogan called back and clicked off the light.

As darkness consumed the room, Brogan looked over at Mr. Squeaks. His colorful face stared lazily ahead. His wide, crooked smile seemed to glow in the light of the moon.

Brogan knew the clown was harmless, but seeing him staring and grinning in the shadows like that was still so bizarre.

So unsettling.

So *scary*.

And that's when Brogan knew his idea to get back at Cammie wasn't just good — it was perfect.

"I'll make her afraid of you," Brogan whispered to the clown. "Then she'll never want to play with you and I won't have to share. Somehow, some way, I'll convince her you're alive!"

FIVE

The next morning, Brogan couldn't wait to get started on his plan.

Unlike his pranks of the past, Brogan knew this one would need to be slow, methodical, and carefully laid out. He couldn't rush it. Not if he really wanted it to work.

First, Brogan needed Cammie to doubt her own reality. He knew the only real way to make her afraid of Mr. Squeaks was to have her start looking at the clown with a suspicious eye. It wasn't as simple as tossing Mr. Squeaks at her or hiding a voice box somewhere in his clothes and making him say crazy things.

No. It had to be mental.

It had to be just enough to get inside of Cammie's *mind*.

And Brogan knew exactly how he was going to accomplish that.

After he woke up, Brogan grabbed Mr. Squeaks from the nightstand and took him into the hall. He quietly tiptoed over to Cammie's room, making sure the coast was clear, and then cautiously peeked inside.

The room was empty.

Brogan snuck into the room and looked around.

Isabella sat on a bench under Cammie's window. Brogan guessed Cammie must've been downstairs having breakfast, as the kitchen and dining room were the only two places Isabella was off limits. And since Cammie always took the doll everywhere she went, it was the only explanation for why she had been left upstairs.

Brogan walked up to Isabella. He plugged his nose as he approached, remembering how much he hated that musty smell she always seemed to emit.

"Ugh," he said as he nudged her over, making room. Brogan placed Mr. Squeaks next to Isabella, laying one of the clown's gangly arms over Isabella's shoulders. Then Brogan stepped back and took a long, studious look at the two of them sitting next to each other.

It wasn't a particularly terrifying visual, but it certainly was strange. And that was all Brogan needed to get things started.

Now, his hardest challenge: to put on the performance of a lifetime.

"*DAD!!*" he shouted and raced out of the room. He hurried down the stairs, tightening his face so he looked angry and upset. "*DAAAAADDDD!!*"

Brogan stormed into the kitchen.

Mr. Fernsby stood behind the island preparing a fruit smoothie. He dropped an orange on the counter when he heard his son calling. "Brogan, what's wrong?"

"*Mr. Squeaks is gone!*" Brogan cried.

"What?" his father asked. "Are you sure?"

"Uh-huh! He's not in my room!"

Brogan looked over at the kitchen table where Cammie sat eating a bowl of Cocoa Pebbles. He narrowed his eyes at her. "You took him, didn't you!?" he asked accusingly.

Cammie dropped her spoon in the bowl and wiped the chocolate milk from her lip.

"Nuh-uh!" she said defensively.

"You're a liar!" Brogan screamed. "You're jealous that I found something you can't have for yourself, so you took him!"

"No, I *didn't*!" Cammie shouted back.

"OK, OK, enough," Mr. Fernsby intervened. He stood between them with both hands raised. Then he gently set a hand on Cammie's shoulder and softly asked, "Cammie, did you take Mr. Squeaks?"

"No!" she answered immediately.

"Are you telling the truth?" he asked.

"Yes!" she cried. "I haven't touched it!"

Mr. Fernsby looked at Brogan and shrugged his shoulders. It was no surprise his dad would believe Cammie's word over his. But Brogan didn't let that stop him.

"I bet he's in your room right now!" Brogan declared. He kept his eyes narrowed and lips pursed, but inside he was beaming.

"No, he's not!" Cammie replied. "In fact, I'll *prove* it to you!"

Cammie pushed her chair out and made a beeline for the stairs. Brogan had to prevent himself from smiling as he hurried to keep up with her.

By the time they reached the top of the landing, Brogan was filled with anticipation. He couldn't wait to see the look on Cammie's face as she entered her bedroom and found Mr. Squeaks sitting on the bench with Isabella. He couldn't wait to see Cammie's confused expression as she wondered how the clown doll got into her room. He couldn't wait to relentlessly blame her for taking him while she questioned what was really happening.

Cammie entered her room and pointed her finger. "See!" she said matter-of-factly. "I *told* you I didn't take him!"

Huh? Brogan scrunched his face in confusion. Then he pushed past his sister and looked into the room.

His jaw dropped.

Isabella sat alone on the bench.

Mr. Squeaks was gone.

SIX

Brogan couldn't believe his eyes. He stepped closer to the bench, checking behind it, then the floor around it.

But Mr. Squeaks was nowhere to be found.

"He — he's gotta be here!" Brogan said desperately. Then he started going through the rest of the room, turning over pillows and blankets, looking behind furniture and moving boxes.

"Stop that!" Cammie shouted.

"He's in here!" Brogan declared. "I know he is!" He tossed a moving box to the side. Something inside the box rattled.

"You're going to break my stuff!" Cammie exclaimed.

A knot of fear twisted in Brogan's stomach. Why wasn't Mr. Squeaks in Cammie's room? Brogan hadn't even been downstairs a couple of minutes! Where could he have gone in such a short amount of time? Who could've taken him?

"*Where is he?*" Brogan mumbled under his breath, his voice just above a whisper.

Then Brogan and Cammie whipped their heads to the sound of footsteps coming down the hall. They both glanced to the open door, just as a figure turned the corner and entered the room.

"There you are!" Mrs. Fernsby said to Brogan as she stepped into Cammie's room. She carried Mr. Squeaks in her arms. "I was just looking for you. I found your little friend here. Any idea how he got in your sister's room?"

Brogan flushed with relief. His internal smile returned, and he immediately jumped back into performance mode, marching forward and taking Mr. Squeaks from his mother.

"I *knew* you took him!" he said to Cammie, his eyes pointed at her.

"But I didn't!" Cammie insisted.

"Don't touch my things anymore!" Brogan demanded. Then, with Mr. Squeaks in his arms, he marched out of Cammie's room and into the hall.

As he walked away, he could hear his mother interrogating Cammie about the doll. "Why did you take something of your brother's? Didn't we teach you not to take things that don't belong to you?"

"But I didn't take him!" she cried. "I don't know what happened!"

Brogan was *actually* smiling by the time he got back to his own room.

His plan had worked. The seed had been planted. And now it was time to move on to Phase Two.

Brogan spent the rest of the day unpacking his things and getting his room together.

As he busied himself putting his collection of books in order on his bookcase, he kept thinking of other things he could do with Mr. Squeaks to scare Cammie.

He figured it was still too soon to do anything *too* crazy. Even with the first prank, Cammie probably wasn't thinking the clown walked *itself* into the room. He knew it was the consistency of each prank — not the prank itself — that would eventually manipulate Cammie into believing what Brogan wanted her to believe.

So, for his next move, he decided to keep it simple and just do a variation of the first prank.

Instead of putting Mr. Squeaks in Cammie's room again, what if he tossed him in the downstairs trash can? Then his parents would see him in there in the morning and think Cammie threw him away in a jealous rage.

If she can't have Mr. Squeaks, no one can.

Yes! It was a great idea!

The rest of the day seemed to drag on forever as Brogan waited for nightfall. He kept himself busy in his room reading an old *Goosebumps* book and munching on pretzel sticks.

Finally, when it was ten past eleven and Brogan was sure everyone had gone to bed, he put his book away and stealthily carried Mr. Squeaks downstairs. The old house creaked and groaned as he made his way to the kitchen. He worried the sounds of the house would alert his parents that he was out of his room and walking around. Luckily, that didn't happen.

Brogan reached his hand up to turn on the kitchen light, then thought better of it. It was too risky on top of all the noise.

Instead, he allowed his eyes a moment to adjust to the darkness before carefully making his way over to the trash can.

He placed Mr. Squeaks inside, allowing the clown's legs and arms to dangle over the lip of the bin.

Next, Brogan sprinkled some of the trash on the floor around the area, just for added effect. Then he stepped back and admired the display.

Brogan smiled, feeling accomplished.

He returned to his room and climbed into bed. Initially, he felt so proud and victorious, but as he lay in the dark staring wide-eyed at the ceiling, unexpected feelings of doubt began to swirl and cloud his mind.

The prank would probably get Cammie in trouble again — that was true. And every part of Brogan wanted to see that. But would this *actually* make her think Mr. Squeaks was alive? That's really what he wanted after all. And why would a living clown doll throw itself into the trash?

The more he thought about it, the more he realized his great idea didn't make much sense.

Brogan sighed. He contemplated going back downstairs and taking Mr. Squeaks out of the trash, at least until he could come up with a better idea.

That's when he heard the squeaking.

SEVEN

Brogan sat up in his bed.

Squeak. Squeak.

The sound was distant and muted, but unmistakable.

Squeak. Squeak.

Brogan climbed out of bed and tiptoed out of his room. As he entered the hall, the squeaks got louder.

SQUEAK. SQUEAK.

The sound was coming from downstairs.

Brogan came to the railing overlooking the foyer. He looked down the dark staircase. No movement from below.

Brogan grabbed the handrail with his clammy hand. It almost slid right off. He wiped his sweaty palm onto his pajama pants. Then he mustered an encouraging breath and started down the stairs.

SQUEAK. SQUEAK.

Thoughts churned in his mind as he reached the foyer. Was there anything else that could be making that noise? It was an old house, that was true, and he expected to hear pipes banging and floors creaking and all the moaning and groaning that comes with living in a house as old as this one.

But *squeaking*?

No.

Because Brogan knew it wasn't the house making that sound.

There was only one thing he could think of that made that noise.

And it just wasn't possible. Was it?

No. He refused to believe it. It just couldn't be true.

The sound was louder than ever as Brogan entered the kitchen.

SQUEAK. SQUEAK. SQUEAK.

Brogan stood in the darkness of the kitchen doorway for what seemed like an eternity. Earlier, he didn't want to turn on the light for fear of getting busted by his parents. But now, with his heart in his throat and a cold chill running down his spine, he didn't want to turn on the light in fear of seeing something he shouldn't.

In fear of something seeing *him*.

But he hadn't come this far for nothing. He needed to know the truth.

Brogan took another deep breath, reached up, and turned on the light.

EIGHT

As light flooded the room, Brogan's eyes darted to the trash can. When he saw what was making the noise, he nervously laughed.

Coco had gotten out of her crate and was chewing on one of the clown's shoes.

SQUEAK. SQUEAK.

The dog tugged and pulled, trying to yank Mr. Squeaks out of the trash without success.

"Coco," Brogan muttered in a relieved whisper. He rolled his eyes and went over to the dog. She was still tugging and pulling on the clown's shoe when Brogan scooped his hand under her belly and picked her up.

"You scared the heck out of me," he said to the dog.

Coco wagged her tail and kissed his nose.

Brogan returned Coco to her crate, making sure the metal door was shut and latched this time. Then he took Mr. Squeaks out of the trash can and went upstairs.

Brogan could hardly keep his eyes open by the time he got back to his room. He tossed Mr. Squeaks by the window and crawled into bed.

He was too tired to come up with another idea to scare Cammie tonight. He'd have to think of something tomorrow.

He fell asleep.

Mr. Fernsby had already left for his first day of work by the time Brogan came down for breakfast.

Mrs. Fernsby had made over-easy eggs and turkey bacon and plated it in the shape of a smiling face. It was Cammie's favorite meal.

Brogan ate quickly, ready to run back upstairs and brainstorm new ideas to scare Cammie.

"Brogan, there was a bunch of trash on the kitchen floor this morning," his mother said as he shoveled food into his mouth. "Any idea how it got there?"

Eyes growing nearly twice their size, Brogan nervously swallowed. Did his mother know what he had been up to last night? Was she testing him?

"Oh, uh — " Brogan searched his brain. "Coco got out of her crate. I heard her downstairs and found her digging through the trash. I thought I picked most of it up. Sorry."

Mrs. Fernsby sighed. "I swear the latch on her crate is broken."

"Yep," Brogan agreed.

"Chalk it up to the usual Fernsby luck," she added sarcastically.

A light bulb suddenly turned on in Brogan's head.

Chalk it up.

He remembered Cammie's walls were painted with chalk paint. What if he wrote something on the wall and made it look like Mr. Squeaks did it?

Cammie would walk into the room and see the writing and Mr. Squeaks with chalk in his hand and totally freak out! Sure, Cammie would probably run downstairs to tell their mom and try to blame *him* for it. But Brogan could erase the writing and remove Mr. Squeaks before his mom ever got a chance to see it for herself.

If he could pull this off, he could scare his sister *and* avoid getting into trouble all at the same time.

The idea gave him a sudden burst of adrenaline.

"May I be excused?" Brogan asked eagerly. His mother nodded, and Brogan left the table and then ran upstairs to his room.

Mr. Squeaks was sitting against the wall under the window. Brogan noticed him and raised a brow. He remembered throwing Mr. Squeaks in that spot last night before bed, but did the doll just happen to land perfectly upright in a sitting position like that? It was strange, but he supposed crazier things were possible.

Brogan picked up the clown and rushed out of his room. He trekked down the hall and into Cammie's bedroom, placing Mr. Squeaks on the floor with his back resting against the wall.

Then Brogan took a red piece of chalk from the tray and scratched his chin.

Hmm, he thought. What to write?

It had to be something short and nasty.

And it had to be something his five-year-old sister knew how to read.

But what?

Brogan took a moment to search the room, looking for inspiration. Nothing seemed to jump out at him.

Until he saw the framed picture of Cammie and her Isabella doll sitting on the dresser.

Brogan smiled. He suddenly knew *exactly* what he was going to write.

He put the piece of chalk up to the wall and started writing. He wrote feverishly and deliberately, making sure the penmanship on the wall didn't match his typical handwriting. He had to make it look like it was done by somebody else.

Brogan completed the last letter, then took a step back to observe his writing:

ISABELLAHATESYOU

Brogan stifled a laugh. This would freak Cammie out for sure! Not only would it make her believe Mr. Squeaks was alive and wrote on her wall, but it would also make her think her own doll — her very favorite thing on the entire planet — didn't even like her back!

It was as brilliant as it was evil. And Brogan couldn't *wait* to see her reaction.

He *had* to record it!

Brogan placed the piece of chalk in Mr. Squeaks' white-gloved hand, rubbing some of the red dust on it for good measure. Then he took off for his bedroom to grab his video camera.

He wasn't prepared for what happened next.

#

When Brogan entered his room and opened the bottom drawer of his dresser, he gasped.

His video camera sat inside the drawer shattered into a dozen pieces. It looked like someone had smashed it with a hammer. Bits of silver and black plastic lied strewn all over the bottom of the drawer in jagged fragments.

Brogan reached down, lifted the tattered piece of technology, and watched as it fell apart in his hands.

"What...no..."

He stood there in silence for several moments, stunned and in disbelief, holding his breath without even meaning to. His eyes darted in their sockets for answers.

How did this happen?

Who could have done this?

And *why*?

Finally, he let out his breath in a long, audible *WHOOSH*. Then he called for the first person that always came to mind whenever something went wrong.

"MOMMMM!!"

Mrs. Fernsby appeared in the doorway within half a minute. "What? What is it?" she asked.

When Mrs. Fernsby saw the remains of her son's camcorder in the drawer, she gasped so deeply, it nearly took all the air out of the room at once. "What — what happened!?"

"My camera broke!" he said.

Mrs. Fernsby tried to pick up the broken remains, but it fell apart in her hands, too. "Brogan, we told you to be careful with this thing!"

"I didn't do it!" Brogan replied defensively.

"Then how did this happen?"

"I don't know!" he answered honestly. "I found it in my drawer like this!"

Mrs. Fernsby's face suddenly turned serious, and she started looking around his bedroom like she was on a hidden camera reality show.

"Brogan, is this another prank?" she asked. "Is your real camera actually okay and this one is fake?"

Brogan wanted to scream. Was she serious!? How could he fake this? He didn't have an arsenal of busted camcorder decoys lying around!

"*NO!*" he shouted, probably louder than he intended. "This is my camera, Mom! And somebody destroyed it!"

"Why would someone do this to your camera?" Mrs. Fernsby asked. It was a good question even Brogan wanted the answer to.

"I don't know!" Brogan said, his voice still shrill and angry.

"OK, OK, just relax," his mother said soothingly. "Let's calm down. There has to be a logical explanation."

"Like what!?"

She scratched her chin, then lifted one finger up as an idea came to her.

"Coco!" Mrs. Fernsby said. "Maybe she came up here and knocked it around by accident. You said she got out of her crate last night."

"Yeah, and after she knocked it around and broke it, she put it back in the drawer!" Brogan rolled his eyes. "Get real, Mom!"

Mrs. Fernsby licked her lips. She wanted to say more to her son, tell him to mind his mouth, but she knew how upset he already was. Instead of adding more fuel to the fire, she bit her tongue and chose to brush it off.

"*It was Cammie!*" Brogan exclaimed, his fist clenched.

"You don't know that," his mother said.

"Yes, I do!" he retorted. "She doesn't want me to have *anything* of my own! Whatever she wants, she takes! And whatever she doesn't get to have for herself, she destroys!"

Brogan motioned for the door.

"Brogan. . ." Mrs. Fernsby reached out to stop him.

"Maybe she needs to know how it feels!" he snapped. "Maybe somebody should break something of hers!"

And that's exactly what Brogan intended to do. He stormed out of the room.

"Brogan, wait!" Mrs. Fernsby took off after him, one hand outstretched but failing to stop him.

But Brogan kept going, his eyes set on Cammie's bedroom, his mind consumed with revenge.

It wasn't until Brogan charged into Cammie's bedroom and saw Mr. Squeaks on the floor that he even remembered what he had needed his camcorder for in the first place.

Oh no, he thought. Now his mom would see Mr. Squeaks on the floor, too. She would see what Brogan had written on the wall for Cammie to find.

His mom would realize he'd been setting up pranks with Mr. Squeaks, and he'd get in trouble for sure.

But his worries turned to fear when he looked at the writing he had left on the wall.

The writing that once said ISABELLA HATES YOU.

The writing that now read:

I HATE YOU

TEN

Brogan couldn't take his eyes away from the writing on the wall — not even when his exasperated mother stormed in behind him and saw the display for herself.

Brogan opened his mouth to say something, but Mrs. Fernsby spoke first.

"I don't believe this," she said quietly.

Brogan watched his mother walk over to Mr. Squeaks and pick him up with one hand. The red piece of chalk fell from the clown's grasp and rolled across the floor.

"I really don't believe this, Brogan," she said disappointedly. "Here I am sympathizing about your camera, and you're only using it to record some ridiculous prank on your sister! I bet you put Mr. Squeaks in Cammie's room yesterday, too!"

Brogan shook his head in frustration. It was true. Everything she said was true. But she didn't know that the writing on the wall had changed. She didn't know something else was going on that even *he* couldn't explain.

"Mom, listen!" he begged. "It's not what you think!"

"No, Brogan!" Mrs. Fernsby exclaimed. "I'm done listening! I'm really tired of this. You've crossed the line this time. You told me you wouldn't play any more pranks! I bet you broke your own camera just to get your sister into trouble. I am so *furious* with you right now!"

Brogan stepped forward, hands splayed, desperate to calm his mother and get her to hear him out.

"Mom, you really don't understand," he said solemnly. "Mr. Squeaks — "

"You can forget about Mr. Squeaks!" Mrs. Fernsby interrupted. "As far as you're concerned, he belongs to your sister now."

Mrs. Fernsby marched for the door, turning back for a final time. "Clean that off the wall before your sister sees. We'll discuss your punishment later."

With Mr. Squeaks in her arms, Mrs. Fernsby left the room.

Brogan felt as hopeless as he did confused. He looked back at the wall, thinking maybe he had psyched himself out in his fit of rage and was just seeing things. Maybe if he looked one more time, the text would be back to the way he had originally written it.

But when he checked again, the haunting red text yielded the truth.

I HATE YOU

How did this happen? he wondered. His dad was at work. Cammie was still downstairs eating breakfast. No one else was upstairs with him and his mom. Not even Coco.

And even *if* Coco had silently come up and accidentally changed the writing by licking a few letters off or brushing against the wall with her fur, it still didn't explain the wrecked camcorder in his drawer, did it?

Nothing about this made any sense!

Brogan reached down and picked up the red piece of chalk from the floor. He returned it to the tray, then took out the eraser and started cleaning the writing from the wall.

When he finished, Brogan went back to his room, sat on the edge of his bed, and stared solemnly at his broken camcorder.

Brogan's thoughts continued to spiral. He realized no one even knew he had placed the camcorder in the drawer in the first place. At his old house, he kept the camcorder on the second shelf of a built-in bookcase in his bedroom. But here? He didn't have that bookcase.

Could his dad have seen him do it when he said goodnight to him? No. He hadn't even come into Brogan's room or opened the door. And what motive would his dad have to destroy the camera, anyway? He was the one who paid for the thing!

Brogan fell onto his back and rubbed his temples. He wanted to clear his mind and dismiss all the intrusive thoughts, but they just wouldn't go away.

Someone must've known the camera was in the drawer.

Someone must've had a reason for destroying it.

But who?

An image of Mr. Squeaks sitting on his nightstand flashed into Brogan's mind.

Mr. Squeaks, who Brogan found in a locked closet.

Mr. Squeaks, whose eyes seemed to follow Brogan no matter which way he went.

Mr. Squeaks, who was in the room when Brogan put the camera in the drawer.

Could it be possible?

Brogan scoffed at the idea. It was such a ridiculous thought. A clown doll coming to life and doing evil little things when no one was looking? Yeah, right!

That's *exactly* what he was trying to get Cammie to believe, and here he was for a brief moment actually entertaining the idea himself!

"You need to chill," Brogan told himself.

Something weird was going on — there was no denying that. But that didn't mean to start going crazy. That didn't mean to start thinking Mr. Squeaks was actually alive.

Right?

ELEVEN

Brogan and his sister started school the next day. Just as he predicted, Brogan was able to see the school bus arrive from his bedroom window.

He was excited about school for a number of reasons. First, Brogan was thrilled he and Cammie would be taking separate buses for the first time ever. He always hated having to share that part of his life with her.

Brogan was also excited to see if any of the kids at his new school would recognize him from his pranking video that went viral. He fantasized everyone staring wide-eyed at him before their jaws hit the floor as they realized who he was. Then he imagined everyone bending over backwards trying to do things for him, hoping to be his new best friend. It really brought a smile to his face thinking about all the attention he would get.

Finally, he was excited about school because it meant getting away for a little while.

Away from the house.

Away from his parents, who were still convinced he was a troublemaker.

Away from his aggravating sister.

And away from Mr. Squeaks, who — despite not wanting to admit it — Brogan hadn't been able to look at the same way since.

Ultimately, no one on the bus recognized Brogan. He figured it was because he was sitting in the very front, so people only got to see a quick glimpse of his face and then the back of his head for the rest of the ride.

But when he finally got to school, he was disappointed no one recognized him there, either.

In class, his teacher, Mrs. Sisino, asked him to stand at the front of the room and introduce himself. But the other kids looked at him like they'd never seen him before. He mentioned the pranking video, thinking he would receive a flurry of "oh yeah!" realizations. Instead, everyone in the class exchanged bewildered glances.

Had they not seen the video? Or had his looks changed that much in the space of six months that they didn't believe it was really him?

It didn't matter. It was clear that Brogan was a nobody here. He felt foolish for thinking otherwise.

At lunchtime, he ate alone. He twirled his spork in his mashed potatoes, too shy to even look up from his tray. Someone walked by as if they were going to sit down with him, but they were only retrieving a rubber band they had accidentally shot across the cafeteria.

By the end of the day, Brogan felt miserable. Nobody talked to him, and he knew going home to his frustrated parents and antagonizing sister wouldn't be any better.

Home and school were indivisible.

As he climbed aboard the bus to go home, he kept his head down and again sat in one of the front seats. Other students piled on, passing by him without so much as a second glance.

Except for one kid in a Minecraft shirt, who stopped in the middle of the aisle and stared at Brogan.

"Hey," the kid said to him, his eyes and mouth agape.

Brogan looked up, unsure if the kid was actually talking to him.

"Uh, hey," Brogan hesitantly said back.

"No way," the kid said under his breath, using one hand to slick his brown hair out of his eyes. Then he repeated himself, but at five times the volume. "No *way*! You — you're Gabriel804!"

A small smile formed on Brogan's face when the kid suddenly took a seat next to him and relentlessly shook his hand.

"I can't believe I'm meeting you!" the kid shouted. He was about Brogan's age, except a little taller and *a lot* louder. "You're like a celebrity! I watch your videos all the time! They're hilarious! I love the one where you sprayed the fart smell in your mom's car, and she thought you pooped your pants. I watched that one twenty times. Hang on, what are you doing on my bus, anyway? I didn't know you were from here!"

The kid had sat down fast, but he talked even faster. His energy was unmatched by anyone Brogan had ever met.

"Thanks," Brogan said, "but I'm not actually Gabriel804. That's my friend's YouTube account. I'm just the guy in the video. My name's Brogan. I just moved here."

"I'm Liam!" the energetic kid responded. "I can't believe you actually ride my bus! This is the craziest thing! Wait, that means you must live in my neighborhood, too! What street do you live on?"

"Old Haven Road," Brogan replied.

"What!? That's my street! Which house is yours? No, wait, don't tell me! It's the one in the cul-de-sac, right? The one where the driveway circles around? I knew it! I live a few houses down from that."

Brogan nodded.

Liam didn't even stop to take a breath. "Wow, this is awesome! We're bus buddies *and* neighbors!"

Brogan could hardly get a word in, but he smiled, nonetheless.

"Listen, Brogan — can I call you Bro? If you need anything, I'm your guy." Liam sat back in the seat as the bus finally closed its doors and began its planned route. "Man, I thought today was going to be trash, but meeting you just made my whole *year*!"

Brogan's cheeks flushed red. This was the exact reaction he hoped to get from all his classmates earlier in the day. He was flattered to be receiving such a reaction from Liam now, but he couldn't imagine how overwhelming it would've been to have gotten this kind of attention from *everyone*.

"I didn't see you on the bus this morning," Brogan noted.

"Doctor's appointment," Liam said quickly. "So when's your next video?"

"Not anytime soon," Brogan responded with disappointment. "My camera broke right after we moved in."

"That's a bummer," Liam replied. "But I guess worse things have happened in that house."

Brogan raised a brow. "What do you mean?"

Liam licked his lips and shook his head. "Nah, I better not. I don't want to freak you out or anything," he said.

"Just tell me," Brogan demanded.

Liam leaned closer to Brogan's ear. "Bro, your new house is evil."

 TWELVE

"Evil?" Brogan could barely repeat the word.

Liam chuckled. "OK, maybe not *evil*," he said with another small laugh. "But the people who lived there before you were really weird."

"Weird how?" Brogan asked.

"You want the full story?" Liam inquired.

Brogan nodded, hanging on to every word.

"Well, this married couple used to live in your house," Liam explained. "They worked for the circus in town. They were both clowns. The wife went by Clarabell, and her husband was the ringmaster. His name was — "

"Mr. Squeaks," Brogan interrupted. And for the first time ever, saying that name out loud sent a cold chill down his spine.

"How did you know that?" Liam asked.

"It doesn't matter," Brogan said and gestured for Liam to go on with the story.

"They also had a son," Liam continued. "He was a trapeze artist. He was really good, too. But one day he had an accident while doing one of his stunts. He fell from the tight rope and died in the middle of a show."

"That's terrible!" Brogan said.

"I know," Liam agreed. "But it gets worse. His parents couldn't handle the loss of their son. They became obsessed with wanting to see him again. And they were willing to do whatever it took to make it happen."

"Like what?" Brogan braced himself as the bus hit a bump in the road.

"They got a fortune teller to come out to the house," Liam revealed. "To perform a séance. They were trying to bring their son back for one final goodbye."

"You're joking," Brogan muttered in disbelief.

"I swear!" Liam responded. "I even saw some of it myself."

"You were there?"

"Not exactly. The night of the séance, I heard strange noises coming from your house," Liam clarified. "And when I looked outside, I could see a green glow coming from one of the upstairs windows."

The bus hit another bump. Behind them, a window slipped free of its latch and dropped down with a deafening clap. Both boys jumped at the sound and then laughed it off.

"So what happened during the séance?" Brogan asked.

"I don't know," Liam answered. "It didn't last long. Something must've scared them off because they ran out of the house, drove off, and never came back."

"They just left all of their stuff?" Brogan couldn't process the idea of moving so suddenly and leaving everything behind.

Liam nodded again. "They never returned to the house themselves, but they had some movers come out a few days later to grab everything."

Not everything, Brogan thought. And an image of Mr. Squeaks flashed in his mind.

Brogan wondered if the Mr. Squeaks doll had anything to do with the family running away in fear.

And if not, there must've been a reason the clown doll was left behind.

In a closet.

In a *locked* closet.

But what could that reason be?

THIRTEEN

That evening, Brogan watched Mr. Squeaks very closely.

Cammie toted him around everywhere she went. It was surprising to everyone in the house since she usually had her Isabella doll glued to her hand. Yet Isabella was nowhere to be found.

When Cammie did her homework in the living room, she made sure Mr. Squeaks was sitting next to her. When Cammie played pretend school upstairs in her bedroom, she played the teacher and made the clown take the position of the student.

Brogan wondered if Cammie really did like Mr. Squeaks that much, or if she was just doing all of this to once again rub it in his face that she had something he didn't. He wouldn't put it past her to be so obnoxious and petty.

But Brogan couldn't prevent his mind from wandering. What if Mr. Squeaks really *was* alive? What if he was somehow manipulating Cammie and taking control of her mind? What if he was secretly earning her trust before forcing her to do things? *Terrible* things? Honestly, if a living clown doll was real, what else was possible?

Brogan forced a laugh. He shook his head and shrugged his shoulders, dismissing the crazy thoughts.

That's really all they were. *Crazy thoughts.*

After all, Brogan hadn't seen anything unusual in his spying all night, so it was silly to continue thinking this way.

It's just a clown doll, Brogan reminded himself.

Still, Brogan wanted to know more about Mr. Squeaks. And not just the doll.

The *real* Mr. Squeaks.

After dinner, Brogan snuck into his parents' bedroom. He swiped the iPad from the nightstand and took it to his own room to start an internet search.

"Mr. Squeaks the clown," Brogan said aloud to the device, watching as the words automatically programmed into the iPad's search bar.

A list of results flashed onto the eleven-inch touchscreen.

Brogan scrolled through the suggested articles. Most of them were news stories about the fatal trapeze accident Liam had mentioned on the bus.

Brogan skimmed through one of the articles, not really getting any new information. It basically summarized what Liam had already told him earlier in the day.

Discouraged, Brogan clicked back and continued scrolling.

Then he stopped.

There was an official link to a circus page called "The Flavio Brothers Circus."

Brogan opened the link.

A picture of the real Mr. Squeaks appeared on the screen. Immediately, Brogan noticed how much the actual man looked like the clown doll. The man had a bald spot on his head, orange hair on the sides, a purple ringmaster suit, and a wide, toothy smile.

Brogan zoomed in on the small caption written beneath the picture: "The Flavio Brothers Circus extends its best wishes and biggest thanks to Mr. Squeaks, who is retiring after thirty years of love, laughs, and squeaks!"

Below that, there was an email address for readers to send fan letters to Mr. Squeaks.

Brogan saw it as an opportunity. Maybe he could reach out to the real Mr. Squeaks and tell him what was going on in the house. Brogan could explain who he was and what was happening with the Mr. Squeaks doll. Perhaps the real Mr. Squeaks would respond with his own experiences, or at least be able to tell Brogan something he didn't already know. It was worth a shot, right?

Brogan checked the date on the website. The picture and caption were posted over two years ago. He wondered if the email address was even active anymore.

Oh well. He had to try. It's not like he had many other options to consider.

Brogan spent the next ten minutes typing his email. He explained how he found the Mr.

Squeaks doll in the locked closet and how he started using it to prank his sister. Then he wrote about his camcorder getting destroyed and the writing on the wall changing on its own.

He concluded the email with a plea for a response, then left his name, phone number, and email address at the bottom. He sent it.

Brogan shut down the iPad and returned it to his parents' room.

He went to bed, his heart racing with anticipation. Would the real Mr. Squeaks receive his email? Would he even read it? And if so, would he respond?

Not knowing the answers to these questions made Brogan jittery and anxious.

He decided to watch a little bit of TV to clear his thoughts before finally turning out the lights and going to sleep.

Brogan woke up to the sound of squeaking. He opened his eyes and turned over in bed, staring into the darkness but not seeing anything.

Squeak. Squeak.

The squeaking was coming from the hallway, just outside his bedroom.

Brogan groaned. Had Coco gotten out of her crate and grabbed Mr. Squeaks again?

SQUEAK. SQUEAK.

The sound was getting louder. *Closer*.

Brogan was about to throw the covers off and investigate the noise when he heard a new sound.

The doorknob jiggling.

He realized there was no way Coco could reach the door handle.

So if it wasn't Coco. . .

Brogan stared wide-eyed, trying to get his eyes to adjust to the darkness but unable to see past the edge of his bed.

He listened as the doorknob creaked and twisted. Then he heard the latch click free and the door slowly creep open.

CRRRREEEEEAAAAAK.

Something stepped into the room.

SQUEAK-THUMP.

SQUEAK-THUMP.

Brogan gasped and pulled the covers over his head. He listened as the squeaking and thumping moved into the room and inched closer to his bed.

SQUEAK-THUMP!

SQUEAK-THUMP!

The sounds continued until whatever was making the noise stopped next to his bed.

Then it got quiet.

Brogan listened, the only sound being his hot breath hitting the bedsheet and blowing back into his face.

He swallowed the lump in his throat, contemplating if he wanted to look or stay under the covers until something provoked him to come out.

But what if nothing happened? What if he stayed under the covers till morning and kept himself awake and afraid for no reason at all?

He decided he had to see.

He had to know the truth.

With unsteady hands, Brogan lowered the bedsheet.

He looked next to the bed.

And gasped when he saw Mr. Squeaks smiling back at him.

FOURTEEN

Brogan screamed!

He jumped out of bed and raced for the door. His shaking hands found the light switch, and Brogan looked back to see if he really saw what he thought he had.

Mr. Squeaks really *was* sitting next to his bed! His eyes hadn't deceived him!

Brogan screamed again.

Suddenly, there was an orchestra of footsteps coming down the hall, and Brogan's door flew open as his parents rushed into the room in a panicked state.

"What is it!?" Mr. Fernsby asked, looking around Brogan's bedroom.

"Honey, are you okay!?" Mrs. Fernsby watched her son latch onto her hip and point to the Mr. Squeaks doll.

"It's him!" Brogan shouted, his voice shrill and terrified. "It's Mr. Squeaks!"

Mr. Fernsby calmly walked over to the clown and picked it up with one hand. He studied Mr. Squeaks for a moment before turning to Brogan with a confused look on his face. "What about him?"

"He. . . he. . ." Brogan could barely speak through his panicked breaths.

"Wait a minute," Mrs. Fernsby said. "What is Mr. Squeaks doing in your bedroom? I thought I made it clear you were *not* to play with him!"

"It wasn't me!" Brogan insisted. "He — he just came into my room!"

"What?" Mr. Fernsby scrunched his face and again looked at the clown doll with a peculiar expression.

"OK, Brogan, this has got to stop," his mother replied. She gently pushed Brogan away and crossed her arms. "Your father and I are really fed up with these jokes."

"It's not a joke!" Brogan declared. "I swear! He just showed up in my room! *By himself!* Please, you have to believe me!" He was practically shouting in desperation.

"Brogan, settle down," Mr. Fernsby said. "You're going to wake up your sister."

Right on cue, as if summoned by the mere mention of her name, Cammie stumbled into the room. "What's going on?" she asked through a heavy yawn as she rubbed the sleep from her eyes.

"Nothing, sweetie," Mrs. Fernsby told her. "Go back to bed."

Before Cammie could leave, Brogan quickly invited her back with his own interrogation. "Cammie, did you put Mr. Squeaks in my room!?"

"Huh-what?" was her sleepy response.

"That's enough, Brogan!" Mr. Fernsby ordered.

But Brogan wasn't giving up that easily. "Mr. Squeaks!" he shouted. "Did you put Mr. Squeaks in my room!? *Tell the truth!*"

Cammie looked at the clown doll hanging from Mr. Fernsby's grasp. Then she innocently shook her head from side to side. "Uh-uh," she said. "It wasn't me."

Brogan's heart sank to his stomach. Secretly, he had been hoping Cammie was the one doing everything with Mr. Squeaks, like moving him into his room in the middle of the night and changing the writing on the wall. Secretly, he was hoping Cammie would confess to all of it, and her declaration of guilt would be a relief from the horrifying truth Brogan didn't want to accept.

But she said no. She *hadn't* put Mr. Squeaks in his bedroom. She hadn't done *any* of the crazy things Brogan had been experiencing.

And he believed her.

It was that confidence in his sister's innocence that confirmed Brogan's irrational fear.

"I didn't do it, either!" he told his family. "That can only mean one thing!""

"What's that?" his father asked.

"He's alive!" Brogan said. "Mr. Squeaks is *alive!*"

FIFTEEN

Brogan's parents looked at him like he was out of his mind.

"I'm telling you the truth!" Brogan insisted. "Mr. Squeaks is alive!"

Mrs. Fernsby rolled her eyes, then took Mr. Squeaks from her husband with one arm and grabbed Cammie's hand with the other.

"Come on, sweetie," she told her daughter as she ushered her to the door. "I'll put you back to bed."

As the girls left the room, Mr. Fernsby looked at Brogan, scratched his scruffy chin, and let out a heavy sigh. "Son, I think we need to talk."

"Dad, I know how it sounds!" Brogan said quickly. "But I'm not lying! He came into my room by himself. I heard him *walking*!"

"Just have a seat," Mr. Fernsby said, sitting on the bed and gesturing for Brogan to join him. It took a few seconds, but Brogan finally unclenched his fist and reluctantly did as he was told.

"Brogan," his father began, "I know moving here isn't what you wanted. You left your school, your friends — *everything*. I know you want to go back. But this is where we are now. Nothing is going to change that. So if you're trying to scare us out of here, it isn't going to work."

"Dad, that's not what I'm doing!" Brogan interjected. "Mr. Squeaks — "

"I'm still talking," Mr. Fernsby said firmly. "These pranks are going to stop — *now*. No more teasing your sister. No more jokes. No more fantasies of dolls coming to life. If I see or hear another thing about Mr. Squeaks or anything else, there are going to be some serious consequences. Do you understand me?"

Brogan closed his eyes and put his chin to his chest. There was nothing he could do to convince his dad he was telling the truth. For years, Brogan had unknowingly dug a hole for himself with every prank he pulled, and now no one would believe him when he really needed them to.

He felt hopeless and defeated.

All he could do was nod. "Yes. I understand."

Mr. Fernsby leaned over and kissed his son on the forehead. "I love you, alright?"

"I love you, too," Brogan said back.

Mr. Fernsby tucked Brogan into bed and turned out the light. He left the room and closed the door.

Brogan lied in bed and stared blankly into the darkness. He knew he wouldn't be asleep anytime soon — not with the crazy, terrifying thoughts of Mr. Squeaks flooding his mind.

The crazy thoughts that suddenly didn't seem so crazy after all.

Mr. Squeaks really *did* change the writing on Cammie's wall.

Mr. Squeaks really *had* walked around on his own.

Mr. Squeaks *was* the one responsible for breaking his camcorder.

That last thought chilled Brogan most of all.

"He broke it so I couldn't prove it," Brogan whispered to himself. "He broke it to protect his secret."

Brogan turned over in bed, more convinced than ever. And the more he thought about everything, the more his fear slowly turned into something else.

Something stronger.

Determination.

"I have to show them," Brogan said to the empty room. "I have to prove to everyone he's alive."

But how?

SIXTEEN

"You're kidding me, right?"

Liam tossed the baseball to Brogan, who — being a leftie — swiftly caught it with his right-handed glove. They were in Liam's backyard and had been tossing the ball back and forth for a good chunk of the Saturday afternoon.

"You don't believe me, either," Brogan said.

"It's not that," Liam replied. "I mean, you even said you thought you were going crazy. And I'm sure you realize that's how all of this sounds to anyone else. *Crazy.*"

"I still feel that way," Brogan confessed. "And that's the scariest part — knowing that I'm not actually out of my mind. This is really happening, Liam. I'm not making this up."

"You're not filming a new prank video right this second, are you?" Liam glanced around his backyard, almost as if expecting a film crew to suddenly jump the fence.

"Now you sound like my mom," Brogan sighed.

Liam could see the look of disappointment on Brogan's face. He softened.

"OK, let's say this doll really is alive," Liam suggested. "How did he come to life?"

"I don't know," Brogan said. "You told me there was a séance in the house. Maybe it had something to do with that." Brogan tossed a curveball.

Liam missed the throw and had to retrieve the ball from the nearby bushes. "So you think the séance actually worked?"

"Maybe." Brogan shrugged.

"That should reassure you a little bit."

"What do you mean?"

"If the séance is responsible for all of this, then at least you know why the doll is alive. The trapeze artist's spirit must be trapped inside of it."

"*That* should reassure me!?" Brogan's eyes practically shot out of his head.

"Of course! Now you know the doll isn't dangerous!" Liam wiped the dirty ball on his jeans and threw it back to Brogan. "The trapeze artist was a nice guy. Totally harmless. So, if his spirit really *is* inside the Mr. Squeaks doll, you shouldn't have anything to worry about!"

"Nothing to worry about!? He broke my video camera!"

"It's just like you said, Bro. He didn't want to be exposed! If you were a spirit trapped in a clown doll, would *you* want people knowing about it?"

"Well, what about changing the writing on the wall? And walking into my room in the middle of the night!?" Brogan could hardly contain his frustration.

"It's not like he was hovering over your bed with a kitchen knife or something!" Liam pantomimed the image. "Maybe he's just trying to communicate with you."

"What could he possibly be trying to say?" Brogan questioned. "Other than the fact that he hates me!"

"I don't think he wrote that," Liam said. "I think he was erasing what you originally wrote and just couldn't finish because you barged into the room."

Brogan pondered this. "So what's he trying to communicate?"

"Maybe he wants to see his parents again. He probably just needs your help to do that."

Brogan thought about this. He silently rolled the baseball in his hand. "What do I do, Liam?"

"The way I see it, you have two options."

"I'm afraid to ask what they are."

"First, you sit with Mr. Squeaks and try to see if he'll talk to you. Maybe you'll get lucky and he'll actually tell you what he wants. Then you won't have to worry about it anymore." Liam raised his open glove, a signal for Brogan to throw the ball to him.

"I don't think my parents will even let me be in the same room as Mr. Squeaks anymore," Brogan said doubtfully.

"Which is why you have the second option."

"What's that?"

"Prove to everyone that he's alive."

"How do I do that?" The image of Brogan's smashed-up video camera flashed in his mind.

"My dad has an old security camera in his garage," Liam revealed. "You could borrow it and try to get footage of Mr. Squeaks coming to life."

"You really think that'll work?" Brogan caught the ball. It hit the inside of his glove with an audible slap.

Liam smiled. "What do you have to lose?"

SEVENTEEN

Liam took Brogan into the garage where he started sifting through old boxes.

"Gotta be here somewhere," Liam said. Then he opened a blue plastic tote and smiled when he saw what was inside. "Aha! Here it is!"

Liam reached into the tote and retrieved his father's old security system. It was a small portable camera on a round, plastic mount.

"How does it work?" Brogan asked.

"It's easy. You hide it somewhere, turn it on, connect it to your Bluetooth, and it automatically sends a live stream to your cell phone."

"I don't have a cell phone," Brogan sighed.

"I do," Liam said cheerfully. "I can watch the footage for you and let you know if anything happens."

"Wait, you're just going to watch a live stream for hours and hours? How are you going to stay awake for that?" Brogan didn't look convinced.

"The app lets you know if there's any suspicious movement," Liam explained.

"Does it record sound, too?"

"I don't think so," Liam replied.

Brogan sighed again. He thought about the sound Mr. Squeaks' shoes had made when he had walked into his bedroom. It would've been ideal to capture that.

"Don't worry," Liam assured him. "No one will need to hear any sounds when they see a clown doll actually moving around on its own."

Brogan smiled. Even if Liam didn't fully believe him, it felt good to have his support. It felt good to be listened to. It felt good to have a friend.

"Thanks, Liam," he said.

Liam returned a grin. "Let's catch a clown!"

* * *

The boys walked to Brogan's house, keeping the security camera hidden in the oversized pocket of Liam's hoodie.

Mrs. Fernsby was in the kitchen when the boys walked inside.

"There you are," she said to her son. "I was just about to come looking for you." Mrs. Fernsby turned her attention to the unfamiliar kid standing in her kitchen. "Hi. I don't believe we've met. I'm Brogan's mom."

"Liam Ellis," he replied.

"Liam lives down the street," Brogan explained. "I thought I told you about him."

"Maybe you did. Listen, your dad's working late tonight, and I have to pick up your sister from gymnastics. You want to stay or tag along?"

"Did she take Mr. Squeaks with her?" Brogan asked.

"Of course she did," Mrs. Fernsby said in a discouraged breath. "You know she takes him everywhere now."

"I'll stay here," Brogan said without a second thought.

Mrs. Fernsby looked at Brogan, a little unsure. "OK. But your friend needs to go home. I don't want anyone over unless I'm here. Sorry, Liam."

"Understandable, Momma Bro."

Brogan made a face at Liam — *really*? Then he looked back to his mother. "Wait, can Liam go upstairs with me really quick? I want to show him something in my room."

"Make it fast, Brogan. I need to leave, and it's going to be dark soon."

"Thanks, Mom!"

"Nice meeting you, Momma Bro!"

Without another word, both boys darted for the foyer and raced up the stairs. When they got to the top, Brogan silently led Liam to Cammie's bedroom and quietly closed the door.

"We'll hide the camera in here," he whispered. "This is where she keeps Mr. Squeaks most of the time."

Liam removed the camera from his pocket and handed it to Brogan. Then he pulled out his cell phone and tapped the preinstalled Security System app.

Brogan placed the camera on a bookshelf, adjusting it so it could get a full view of the room. Then he slid a book over to try to hide the camera without blocking the lens.

"You don't think she'll see it, do you?" Liam asked.

"I don't think so," Brogan replied.

Together, the boys looked at Liam's phone and watched the video feed. It offered a perfect view of the room. There was no way it would miss anything.

"It's perfect," Liam said.

"This is really going to work," Brogan agreed. And both their faces lit up with excitement.

They didn't know that, by the end of the night, their excitement would turn to terror.

EIGHTEEN

Liam left for home, and Mrs. Fernsby drove to pick up Cammie from gymnastics shortly after that.

For the first time, Brogan had the house to himself.

Well, not counting Coco.

He wanted to be more excited about it, but being alone in a house with nothing but scary experiences so far wasn't exactly something to look forward to.

The sun was already setting on the horizon. It would be dark in minutes. His mother instructed him to pull the shades on all the windows while she was gone. He never understood why that was important, but he went about the house and did it anyway.

Brogan hesitated when he got to Cammie's bedroom. He remembered finding Mr. Squeaks on the floor and the words I HATE YOU written on the wall above him.

But thinking about that now was silly. Mr. Squeaks wasn't even in the house. He had no reason to be afraid of anything.

Brogan entered the bedroom and pulled the curtains closed. He glanced at the far wall, almost expecting those mean-spirited words to still be there.

But the wall was blank.

Brogan let out a reassured sigh and left the room.

His mother and sister weren't due back for about an hour, so Brogan figured he didn't have much time to do anything he really wanted to. He thought about trying to hack the parental controls on the TV and watch something he wouldn't normally get to watch, but by the time he figured it all out, they'd probably return before he could actually get away with watching anything.

Brogan plopped onto the couch and put his feet up.

There was a knock on the door.

Brogan perked up to the sound. Who could be visiting at this hour? It was already dark outside.

The knocks came again.

Louder.

Harder.

Brogan cautiously rose from the couch and tiptoed to the front door. He had been taught all his life not to answer the door when his parents weren't home, and he didn't forget that now as he double-checked to make sure the deadbolt was locked.

The knocking came again, so strong this time that a framed picture on the wall shook on its nail.

"Bro!?"

He paused. Brogan recognized that voice immediately. "Liam?"

"Yeah, it's me! Open up! Hurry!"

Brogan slid the deadbolt over and opened the door for his friend. Liam impatiently rushed into the house and jumped up and down with excitement.

"What's going on?" Brogan asked. "You're not supposed to be here, remember?"

"*We've got something!*" Liam shouted.

"Huh?"

"The footage!" Liam held out his phone for Brogan to see.

But Brogan wouldn't even look. He shook his head and threw up his hands in a gesture of confusion. "Liam, what are you talking about? My mom hasn't even come back from picking up my sister yet. Mr. Squeaks isn't even here!"

"Well, this footage says otherwise!" Liam held up the phone again, and Brogan actually looked this time. But all he could see was a solid black screen with a red dot blinking in the corner.

"I don't see anything," Brogan said.

"It's because the light in the room is off," Liam clarified. "But do you see that red dot blinking on the top right? That means the camera detects movement in the room!"

Brogan let out a small laugh. "It's because I was just in the room, Liam. I was closing the curtains."

But Liam's eager, serious expression didn't change.

"Bro, this isn't a recording," he said. "It's still live streaming. And that red dot is still blinking."

"What are you saying?"

"Something is moving in that room — *right now!*"

NINETEEN

"That's impossible!" Brogan shouted. "You heard my mom! She said Cammie took Mr. Squeaks with her to gymnastics!"

"Are you sure about that?" Liam asked. "Earlier, your mom didn't seem to remember you ever mentioning me. Maybe she was wrong."

"I think my mom would remember seeing a clown doll in her car," Brogan replied.

"Maybe she *did* take him," Liam suggested. "And maybe Mr. Squeaks came back on his own!"

"Without anybody noticing?" Brogan was doubtful. There had to be another explanation.

Brogan's eyes drifted over to one of the pictures on the wall. It was a picture of the whole family, including —

"Coco!"

"What?"

"My dog! She's probably up in Cammie's room right now! That's why the red dot is blinking! She's probably bouncing around like crazy up there!"

"You mean *that* dog?" Liam pointed as Coco trotted into the foyer from Mr. Fernsby's office. She licked Liam's pant leg and moved on to the living room.

Brogan and Liam both looked each other, then at the phone screen.

The red dot was still blinking.

"There's no way," Brogan muttered in disbelief. "It's just not possible!"

"Only one way to find out." Liam gestured to the stairs.

A wave of apprehension washed over Brogan. He didn't want to go upstairs. His heart was pounding so hard in his chest, he thought it would bounce off his ribs and explode out of his back. The fear was just too much to handle.

And with fear taking control, Brogan started stalling.

"You're not supposed to be here," he desperately reminded Liam. "My mom will be home soon. I'll get into *so* much trouble if she sees you!"

"Bro, do you *really* want me to leave you alone knowing there's something else in your house?"

Brogan's face flushed. Liam was right. There was no way he wanted to be left alone in this house with something moving around upstairs.

He was terrified of finding out what it was, but the more he thought about it, *not* knowing scared him even more.

He didn't have a choice.

"OK," Brogan nervously agreed. "Let's go see."

Together, the boys ascended the stairs. They stepped quietly, trying not to make a sound, but the old steps still creaked beneath their weight.

Liam's eyes stayed on the phone screen.

The red dot was still blinking when they reached the top of the landing. They moved in on Cammie's closed bedroom door. Brogan wondered if he had closed the door on his way out from shutting the curtains. Maybe he had. He couldn't remember.

"Wait," Liam whispered. "The dot just stopped blinking."

Brogan looked at the door, then back at Liam. "What do we do?"

"We can't back out. Open it on three?" Liam shrugged and put the phone in his pocket.

Brogan nodded and started to count.

"One. . ."

He reached for the doorknob.

"Two. . ."

He grabbed it and turned.

"Three!"

In perfect sync, Brogan and Liam slammed their shoulders into the door and barreled into the room.

Brogan clicked on the light.

When they saw what was waiting for them, their jaws dropped.

TWENTY

"No — *NO!*"

Brogan and Liam both backed away, their eyes scanning the room and taking in the writing scribbled all over the wall.

I HATE YOU

It was back! Written everywhere, dozens of times in various colors and sizes. Pieces of dull chalk decorated the floor.

"*No, no, no!*" Brogan repeated. "It can't be!"

Liam looked around the room, but there was no sign of Mr. Squeaks, or anything else.

"How?" Brogan asked, his voice shakier than ever. "*How?*"

"There's nothing in here," Liam said. "It's just us!"

"What is going on!?" Brogan collapsed against the wall.

"I — I don't know!" Liam replied, and his voice quivered, too.

They were both as terrified as they were confused.

"Let's calm down for a minute," Liam said, regaining control. "There's a reason for this. There has to be. We just have to think."

"Think? *Think!?*" Brogan stood tall and laughed nervously. "I can't *think* anymore, Liam! I can't handle any of this!"

"Relax!" Liam told his friend. "We're going to figure this out!"

"Figure *what* out!? I'm living in a house where clown dolls walk around on their own and chalk writing appears out of nowhere! The house is haunted, Liam! There's no other explanation!"

"You don't know that for sure!" Liam said, his voice getting louder. "It could be something else!"

"Like what!?"

"I don't know, Bro! This is all crazy! How do I know *you* didn't write that on the wall before I came over here!?"

"What!? No way! Why would I do that!?"

"Because that's what you do, Bro! You play pranks on people!"

"I wouldn't do that to you, Liam! You're my friend! And even if I did, that still doesn't explain why something was moving around in here when I was downstairs with you!"

That's when they heard it.

A tapping sound. Like a marble rolling.

No.

Not a *marble.*

They looked down in time to see a red piece of chalk roll out from under the bed and come to rest against Brogan's foot.

Brogan picked it up and showed it to Liam. Then their eyes drifted to Cammie's bed where the sheer bed skirt fluttered and rippled.

They both stared, paralyzed with fear.

"There — there's something under the bed," Brogan choked out.

They looked at each other, then back at the bed.

"I have to know," Brogan said. And with a reassuring breath, he started towards the bed.

"Bro, don't!" Liam tried to pull him back, but Brogan continued forward. He reached the foot of the bed and got down on his knees.

With a trembling hand, Brogan slowly reached for the bed skirt. He was about to grab hold of it and lift it up when he pulled his face away and plugged his nose.

"Ugh," he said. "That smell!"

"What smell?" Liam asked.

Brogan said nothing, even though he knew *exactly* what the smell was. It was a smell he had to deal with every day of his life. It was a smell he hated more than anything else in the world.

Brogan looked back at the bed, and that's when he saw it.

The face.

Staring back at him through the sheer bed skirt.

It was a face that looked like the Mona Lisa. A face he had seen a million times before.

But for the first time, it was a face that looked directly at him and smiled.

"Hello, Brogan," the face said.

Without warning, a plastic hand shot out at Brogan from under the bed.

He gasped and jumped back, crab-walking backwards until he bumped into Liam, who helped him to his feet.

"What is it!?" Liam asked.

Brogan didn't have a chance to answer.

They watched in silent horror as a two-and-a-half-foot doll named Isabella crawled out from under the bed and stood up on her own.

TWENTY-ONE

Isabella stepped forward, and as she did, Brogan and Liam stepped back.

"Isabella. . ." Brogan blinked several times, trying to process what he was seeing, but the only way he could convince himself it was really happening was to say it out loud. "You — you're alive!"

"That's right," the doll said, her voice light and feminine but with a raspy undertone. "You didn't forget about me, did you?"

Suddenly, there was a loud bang. Brogan looked next to him. "Liam?"

Liam had fainted.

Isabella looked down at Liam's motionless body. Then she narrowed her eyes at Brogan, her tiny mouth snarling.

"You're not the first to forget about me, Brogan. Your sister forgot me, too. She forgot me because of *you*!"

"I. . . I. . ." Brogan struggled for words that just wouldn't come.

"*I* was her favorite," Isabella declared. "I've *always* been her favorite. But then you tried to change that. You told her I hated her! You tried to make her hate *me*!"

Brogan remembered writing ISABELLA HATES YOU on the wall.

"I could never hate her!" Isabella revealed. "Not the way I hate *you*!"

Brogan looked around the room, seeing the words written all over the walls.

I HATE YOU

"You've been doing all of this," Brogan realized. "*You* wrote on the wall! *You* broke my video camera! *You* put Mr. Squeaks in my room!"

Isabella grinned. It was a grin of self-accomplishment.

"Why?" Brogan asked.

Isabella's face turned solemn and serious. "Why do you think I did it? Cammie would've never gotten Mr. Squeaks for herself if it weren't for your stupid pranks! And I'd still be her favorite!"

Isabella marched forward, her movements stiff and unnatural.

"*Nobody* forgets Isabella!" she said.

Brogan backpedaled away from her, his mind searching for an idea.

"You think doing all of this is going to make Cammie remember you?" Brogan laughed. "You think she's just going to forget about Mr. Squeaks and come back to you?"

Isabella's eyes narrowed even more. Brogan could see he had struck a nerve with her.

"News flash, you plastic psycho! Cammie doesn't want you anymore! No one in this family wants you! You're ancient history! Nothing you do will make her remember you, so you might as well give it up and get out!"

Brogan was panting by the time he finished talking. He took a moment to catch his breath.

Isabella just stood there, her face cold and expressionless.

"No," she said flatly. "That's not what I want."

Brogan didn't understand. "Then what do you want?"

He held his breath as Isabella's painted lips curved into a mischievous smile.

"To ruin your life," she said with evil glee. "To ruin your life the way you've ruined mine!"

Then, with a high-pitched screech unlike anything Brogan had ever heard before, Isabella charged at him.

TWENTY-TWO

Brogan instinctively grabbed the security camera from Cammie's shelf and tossed it at Isabella. It hit the doll in the chest and knocked her back.

"AGGHH!!" she screamed.

Brogan didn't waste a moment. With Isabella down, he ran out of the room.

Brogan raced down the hall and got to the stairs. He started down them as fast as his legs would carry him, bypassing some steps and taking most of them two at a time.

When he reached the bottom, he heard a sound from above and looked up.

Isabella was back on her feet and had already climbed the upstairs railing overlooking the foyer. Without a chance to react, Brogan watched as she jumped from the handrail and fell directly on top of him, clinging to his back and clawing at his shoulders.

"AHHH!! GET OFF ME!!" Brogan twisted and turned and tried to do everything he could to rid himself of the doll. But Isabella clung tightly, her plastic fingers digging into his skin.

Brogan winced and fell to the ground.

"You think you can get rid of me!?" the doll hissed, still scratching at his back. "I'll get rid of you first! You think anyone will miss *you*!?"

Isabella bit down on his shoulder. Brogan yelped in pain.

Then she reached for Brogan's face. Her fingers raked across his cheeks.

"LET ME GO!!" he cried.

Suddenly, Brogan felt the weight of the doll abruptly disappear. Confused, he looked up and saw Liam towering over him, holding the manic doll by her hair. The doll shrieked and slashed her hands and kicked her feet, not able to free herself from Liam's grip.

Liam whipped the doll around in a circle, then flung her into the living room. She hit the floor with a heavy thud and skidded against the wall.

"Bro, are you okay!?" Liam helped his friend to his feet.

"Yeah, I think so." Brogan rubbed his pained shoulder and looked at Liam with concern. "Are *you* okay?"

"Yeah," Liam said. "Sorry I passed out. That was the freakiest thing I've ever seen."

"No kidding. Thanks for saving me."

"I haven't saved you yet."

Both boys looked at the living room, ready to face their opponent for a final showdown.

But Isabella was no longer on the floor against the wall.

Brogan's eyes bulged.

"Where — where'd she go?"

TWENTY-THREE

The boys advanced into the living room, their eyes scanning the floor for any sign of the doll. But the room appeared to be empty.

"Do you see her?" Brogan asked.

Liam shook his head. "She's gotta be in here somewhere!"

Brogan heard a sound by the fireplace. He looked that way and then tugged at Liam's sleeve.

"Liam, look." He pointed.

Liam followed Brogan's finger to the fireplace tool set. The tools were gently clanging together, as if they were just touched by something unseen.

"The fire poker," Brogan noted. "It's gone!"

"Oh, *great!*" Liam marched over to the fireplace tool set and grabbed the shovel for himself. He held it like a baseball bat. "Well, two can play at that game!"

Brogan pulled at his hair. "You really think a shovel stands a chance against a fire poker!?"

"We'll see about that!" said a raspy voice coming from directly behind them.

Hesitantly, the boys turned.

Isabella was standing by the armchair wielding the fire poker. She let out a banshee battle cry, raised the poker, and ran at the boys, full speed.

"Ohh!" they gasped.

But Isabella only made it a few steps when she was suddenly, unexpectedly knocked to the ground. The fire poker flew out of her hand and slid across the room as Isabella's assailant pinned her to the floor.

"Get it off me!" the doll cried.

Brogan smiled ear to ear when he saw what was happening. He put his hands to his mouth in the shape of a megaphone and shouted, "*Get her, Coco!*"

The Boston Terrier chomped down on Isabella's face and furiously shook her back and forth. The doll's body twisted and contorted, slapping violently against the floor. One of her arms pinwheeled and then flew out of its socket.

"*Good girl, Coco!*" Brogan cheered.

The dog placed a paw on Isabella's chest. Then, with the doll's head in her mouth, Coco tugged as hard as she could.

Isabella's head popped free.

Brogan and Liam whooped and hollered as Coco rolled Isabella's severed head in her jaws.

The doll's headless body went limp.

And just like that, Isabella was no more.

The boys worked fast to clean everything up before Brogan's mom and sister returned home.

Brogan went upstairs to Cammie's room and cleaned all the writing off the wall. Then he pocketed the security camera to return to Liam.

Downstairs, Liam put the fire poker and shovel back on the rack. Then he placed the dismembered Isabella doll in a black trash bag he found under the kitchen sink.

Together, the boys went into the detached garage and tossed the tied-off bag into the trash can. They closed the lid and exchanged reassured smiles.

"We're not going to tell anyone about this, are we?" Liam asked, but it didn't come out as a question.

"No way," Brogan agreed. "Who would believe us, anyway?"

Liam left Brogan's house shortly after that, just as Mrs. Fernsby's car pulled into the driveway. Liam hid behind a sugar maple so she wouldn't see him, and then, when the coast was clear, he ran the rest of the way home.

At the front door, Brogan greeted his mom and sister, the latter of whom was carrying Mr. Squeaks in her arms.

"Hey," he said to his sister. "How was gymnastics?"

"Fine," she said, giving him a strange look. Brogan had never asked her a question like that before. Right away, she knew something was up. "What's going on?"

"Uh, something happened while you were gone," Brogan revealed.

"What?"

"Coco found Isabella." He held up Isabella's detached head. It was the one piece of the doll he hadn't tossed into the trash bag.

Cammie looked at the doll's head. Isabella's face was caved in and decorated with bite marks. She was hardly recognizable.

Surprisingly, Cammie didn't seem too bothered by it.

"That's okay," she said.

"You're not mad?"

"Nah. Isabella was getting kind of clingy, anyway."

Brogan paused at this remark. Did Cammie know Isabella was alive this whole time?

"Besides," Cammie continued, "I've got Mr. Squeaks now. He's *way* cooler."

Brogan nodded. "Yeah," he agreed. "He's pretty cool."

* * *

Brogan was crawling into bed when he heard the house phone ring. He figured it was his dad calling from work, so he was surprised when his mother brought the cordless into his bedroom and said it was for him.

"Who is it?" he asked his mother.

"Not sure," she said. "Maybe your friend from down the street?"

Brogan took the phone and waited for his mother to leave the room. Then he spoke into the transmitter. "Hello?"

"Hello," a voice replied. "Is this Brogan Fernsby?"

"Yes, it is." Brogan didn't recognize the voice and narrowed his eyes trying to place it.

"My name is Clive Collingwood," the voice revealed. "But you may know me as Mr. Squeaks."

Brogan's eyes lit up. "Oh. Yeah. Of course."

"I apologize for calling so late," the real Mr. Squeaks said. "But I got your email and had to contact you right away."

Brogan facepalmed. He totally forgot he had sent that email to this guy. How was he going to explain what *really* happened?

"Yeah. Uh. Listen." Brogan swallowed the lump in his throat and searched his brain for the right words. "I don't think I should have sent that email to you. This is going to sound insane but I found out — "

"Brogan, is the Mr. Squeaks doll still in your house?" the man interrupted.

"Uh, yeah," he said. "My little sister has him."

"Listen to me very carefully," the man said. "I want you to take the doll away from your sister. And I want you to get it out of the house. *Right now.*"

Brogan nervously laughed. "What's going on?"

"The doll isn't just a doll," the man revealed. "There's something inside of it."

Brogan recalled the séance Liam had mentioned on the bus. "Your son's spirit," Brogan uttered under his breath.

"No," the man replied. "We tried to contact our son. We wanted his spirit to use the Mr.

Squeaks doll to speak to us. But something else found its way inside the doll first."

Brogan's face turned white. "Something else?"

"Something dangerous," the man said. "Something *inhuman*. We tried destroying the doll. We drowned it in the bathtub. We threw it in the fireplace. Nothing worked. That's why we kept it locked in the closet. We didn't know how else to contain the horrible thing within it."

Brogan couldn't speak. His vocal cords froze in his throat.

"Brogan, are you listening to me? Don't let it anywhere near you or your sister! Do you hear me? You're in grave danger! Brogan? *Brogan!*"

Brogan absently dropped the phone. It hit the floor with a deafening clank.

He sat rooted to his bed, paralyzed with fear. That's when the bedroom door suddenly swung open, and Cammie exploded into the room with the biggest smile on her face.

"Brogan!" she said excitedly. "You're never going to believe this! It's absolutely incredible! Mr. Squeaks does a trick!"

Brogan opened his mouth to say something, but again his vocal cords failed him.

Cammie quickly took a seat next to Brogan and rubbed her hands together in anticipation.

"Watch — you're going to *love* this!" Cammie drummed her hands against her legs and called out, "Alright, Mr. Squeaks, show us your trick!"

"Cammie, no. . ."

But it was too late.

Brogan looked at the open doorway and listened to the sound emerging from the other end of the house.

A series of thumping, squeaking footsteps approached from the far end of the hall.

Walking.

Running.

"Here he comes!" Cammie said with an eager smile.

SQUEAK-THUMP!

SQUEAK-THUMP!

SQUEAK-THUMP!

Twisted enough to handle more?

Stay **SHOOK** with another
creepy cursed caper...

A BLESSING IN DISGUISE

By Cameron Munson

For Gramma
Thanks for always finding the magic.

November 1st was Maggie's least favorite day of the year. She had always felt as though all of the multicolored leaves made their final descent the evening before while she was out trick-or-treating — and with them they took the last spell of magic the year had to offer.

But this Halloween was different. Not only was it on a Saturday — which was a true blessing — but the moon's majestic and silvery shadows guided Maggie and her best friend, Amy, on their way through the cobblestoned neighborhood in the center of town.

Her mother, Emily, died when Maggie was eight, but she always felt gently enveloped in her mother's comfort on Halloween — for Halloween was also her mother's birthday.

Dressed in her fantastic homemade witch costume and enjoying the festivities to the fullest, Maggie thought often of her mother that Halloween. When her mother was here in the living and not the spirit world, they would spend the entire month of October creating decorations from cardboard and mixing wax and flowers for candles while Talia, her other mom whom she called Ma, brewed fresh cider with cloves.

The morning sun was already melting the frost at the corners of her windows when she rolled over and opened her eyes. How glorious to lazily wake up and not rush off to school today.

She dressed and traipsed down into the kitchen where she found Ma gazing out the window into the dense oaks and colorful maple woods behind their home.

"Good morning, sweet pea," Ma cooed as she raised a steaming mug of tea.

"Good morning, Ma," Maggie said as she cut a slice from the loaf of pumpkin bread on the table.

"It's absolutely gorgeous outside. You should take a walk and gather more pinecones for our holiday centerpiece." Ma sliced a piece of bread as well.

"Mmm, that sounds nice. I'll take Petey with me," Maggie said as she looked under the table to find Petey licking crumbs off the floor.

The *crunch-swish-crunch-swish* of leaves beneath her feet was soothing as they set out towards the pines at the far edge of the woods. Petey loved jumping and rolling around in the piles, his golden fur shining through.

As usual, almost all of the leaves had fallen in the night, and the sunshine was poking through the branches to keep them warm enough for their journey.

Ma was right; it was absolutely gorgeous outside. Maybe this wouldn't be such a bad November 1st after all.

At the edge of a clearing there were bushels of windswept leaves. Maggie tumbled backwards and a confetti of orange pillowed around her. She couldn't hear Petey rustling around, so she let out a quick whistle, and in an instant, he jumped towards her from inside the mound of leaves, causing an eruption of laughter.

Petey had wandered into their backyard from the woods one day — as if by magic. Maggie was washing dishes at the kitchen window when she noticed his fluffy gold tail peeking up from around the deck. She had wanted a dog for as long as she could remember, but she never expected one to just appear in her backyard. It was impossible that it could be a neighbor's dog. Their acreage was vast, and it took nearly an hour of winding through the countryside just to get to the center of town. The land had been passed down for generations, and Emily and Talia had been the only ones in the entire town to refuse to sell. Mother had always told Maggie that it was sacred.

Ma had her own ways of showing Maggie how bountiful it was. One summer an entire garden of fruits and vegetables sprouted out of nowhere. And then, one day, a few months after Emily had passed on, Petey arrived.

He felt like a gift from the woods themselves. He didn't require any training, and it was as if he had known Maggie and Ma their entire lives.

After playtime in the leaves, a gust of wind picked up and pushed them back into the trees. Petey bounded far ahead to where Maggie almost lost sight of him. She yelled for him to wait up when suddenly she tripped on something and tumbled forward — landing hard on the palms of her hands. The ground felt hot to the touch, as if it had been baking in the sun.

She scrambled to her feet and realized she had tripped into a shallow pit of some sort. Petey had come bounding back to her rescue and nuzzled her wrists.

"What in the heck?" Maggie stepped out of the pit and grabbed at the vines and years of moss and muck that layered the weather worn stone. It was definitely a pit of some sort. A fire pit? Way out here in the middle of their woods? How had she never come across this before?

She took a deep breath, and as she exhaled, the sound of leaves blowing in the wind above her took her by surprise. She looked up to find a circle of tree branches around her, all decorated in maroons and oranges and browns. Last night's frost seemed to have touched all of the trees in the forest except for those surrounding this mysterious pit. And why was the ground inside hot to the touch?

She knelt down, and Petey sat next to her. She extended her hand to touch the ground within the circle again. Definitely hot, but that didn't make any sense. She felt the grayish green stone that made up the pit, and it too was hot, but more like the hearth of a fireplace.

132

As she embraced the warmth of the stones, a sudden and soaring flash of flame shot up from the center of the pit.

Maggie and Petey both scrambled back and looked at each other — wide eyed. Surely that couldn't have just happened.

Then, a female wailing, emitting from a deep and guttural place within the pit, struck them. Maggie covered her ears while Petey tried to cover his with his paws. When the piercing cry stopped, it was as if the forest went absolutely silent.

Frightened, Maggie began to run towards the house, Petey leaping beside her. The only sound she was able to hear was her own beating heart.

They burst through the back door. "Ma!" Maggie cried into the empty house. "Ma, where are you?" Then she noticed a yellow sticky note on the counter:

Went to the farmers market, and then to have lunch with a friend. Be back by 4. Please clean your room. Love you!

Great, now she was alone until it got dark with some wailing woman hiding in the woods and a cursed stone fire pit that randomly burst into flames whenever it wanted.

Cursed, could that really be?

She looked down at Petey who made a pitiful whine. "I know, boy," she said and gave him a biscuit. He crunched it down and padded over to his large bed by the door. In a moment, he was asleep.

Determined to figure out what was happening in her own backyard, Maggie warmed up some soup in the microwave to put in her thermos, grabbed a notebook and pencil, her Polaroid camera and opened her satchel.

While the soup warmed, Maggie was reminded of a time when her mother had taken her to the brook on the other side of the house. Emily had told Maggie that as long as she lives here, the woods would be forever changing — forever inviting her to find something new. While Maggie playfully dipped her hands in the cool water, she came across a small frog and was enamored with its cuteness. Emily helped her daughter cradle the creature, and they had laughed and laughed as it talked to them in its foreign tongue.

Now, as Maggie was thinking about her mother's words of an ever-changing forest, she certainly did not expect to uncover a fire-breathing pit in the middle of their woods. She would have preferred some more adorable animals.

Maggie could see the wind picking up outside, and she added a scarf around her neck. Petey was lightly snoring as she closed the door behind her.

Between the full moon last night, daylight savings, Halloween on a Saturday, *and* missing her mother — maybe it was all just a little too much for Maggie to process. She had stayed up way later than usual too, because —

why not? How often is Halloween on a Saturday? That must be it; she was just tired and imagining things.

But Petey had seen and heard it all, too. And she had always trusted Petey's senses.

As soon as Maggie reached the fire pit, the sun formed a circle of light around it. The sunshine gleamed around the edges of the autumn colored leaves still on their branches and sparkled on the stone pit.

She took the items from her satchel, grabbing her camera last and snapping a photo of the fire pit. While she waited for the photo to expose, she took a large gulp of soup, warming her. Then she took out her notebook and jotted down the strange experience from earlier as she leaned against the stone pit. It was warm against the small of her back, soothing, and she eased into it as she wrote.

Leaves began to fall gently as the temperature in the air slowly rose. Just as a bright yellow leaf landed on her open notebook, a crackling began inside the pit.

Then she heard whimpering, from a woman.

She stood and looked around — seeing no one. Then, the gruff bellows of angry men. Turning left and right but not laying eyes on a soul, Maggie was perplexed.

That's when the crackling swelled into an overwhelming whoosh as fire burst inside the pit — the heat knocking Maggie backwards. An ember leapt out of the pit and onto Maggie's single Polaroid photo. She snatched it as the woman's helpless yet undecipherable cries continued, and the men got more angry. She shook the ember from the photo and gasped at what the exposed photograph revealed.

A woman, dressed plainly in a worn robe and oversized hood, and a handful of men in strangely shaped black hats holding torches crowded the fire pit.

Maggie let the photograph fall to the forest floor, and when she looked up, she shook with fright. Two men were tying rope to bind the woman's hands and feet to a post while a third tied a rope around her mouth!

This is really happening!

Horrified, Maggie wanted to rush to help the woman, but the heat was a dangerous barrier and wouldn't let her advance. She watched in absolute horror until the woman tilted her head back and looked directly at Maggie.

Impossible! Maggie thought. She can't see me, there's no way!

But she did. And as she looked at Maggie, Maggie suddenly felt overwhelmed with a sense of comfort, and love. Maggie rubbed her eyes, and when she reopened them, the woman was now looking above to the circle of bright autumn leaves. One of the men tossed his torch into the center of the pit, and all the men stepped back. The men grumbled nasty things to each other, making the hairs on the back of Maggie's neck stand up.

What horrible, evil men!

The woman's robe caught fire first, but she stopped whimpering and began muttering something.

"Curses! She's speaking curses!" yelled one of the men. With the rope in her mouth it was entirely undecipherable, but Maggie heard the woman's voice clearly in her head.

"Shall all anger and resentment become understanding and light. May those with vibrant and gentle spirits lay a hand to rest on those of opposite afflictions. Shall the light of the silver moon guide you upon your journey to your true self. May all who wander here in this wood grow wild and pure, and feast upon an endless bounty. May the warmth of this fire bestow upon me everlasting peace and make me not afraid, for I too shall return to dust."

The woman laid her head towards her chest in peace, and strands of auburn hair danced out from beneath her hood and into the heat.

Tears streamed down Maggie's face as she choked back sobs. She'd known this land had been in her family for over three hundred years, and of course living in New England she had heard about the witch trials, but to discover that an actual witch burning had happened here? She allowed herself to sob for another moment and when she opened her eyes the image of the woman and the men, and the fire slowly started to fade away.

As soon as their images were gone, all the leaves above the fire pit began to gently fall around her. It was mesmerizing. Hundreds of leaves in orange and purple and brown and yellow twirled around her, tickling her nose and ears as they fell. Maggie's auburn hair, like that of the witch who burned, blew softly in a breeze falling from above.

She walked over to the fire pit and placed her palm gently on the soil inside, to say thank you. She understood. What others may have seen as a curse was simply a blessing in disguise. The witch from many years ago bestowed a gift upon Maggie and her family and the land on which she was raised. There was enough darkness surrounding the world already, but this woman, in her dying moments, placed a blessing upon them, letting it be known that light always overcomes darkness.

Maggie gathered her things and threw her satchel over her shoulder. She could see the rising moon beginning its evening reign as she walked through the trees to the house.

Petey was waiting at the door for her, and she knelt down and gave him a big kiss on his nose. She removed her shoes and took a seat at the table.

What a day! She took out the Polaroid photo and looked at it, surprised. The photo was not of the fire pit, like she had taken. Nor was it of the woman and the men and fire.

It was of her mother, holding her pregnant belly and smiling upwards towards the sky.

ABOUT THE AUTHORS

C.S. JAMES is a former Pre-K teacher and current horror fanatic. He loves Halloween and anything creepy (well, except roaches). Besides being the creator of *Twisted Books to Leave You Shook*, he's had several screenplays produced into spooky short films. *Toy Horror Story* is his second book.

CAMERON MUNSON has been a creature of the night and lover of all things spooky since he learned how to walk. For one of his first trick-or-treats, he dressed up as a witch — complete with a fancy necklace and pair of his mother's clip-on earrings. For all those reading, he sends his deepest thanks. To thine own self, be true!

SCARES THAT CARE is a 100% volunteer organization focused on fighting REAL MONSTERS of childhood illness, burns, and breast cancer. They help families who are experiencing hardships cope with the financial burden by raising and providing $10,000 per recipient family. Please consider donating and supporting this incredible cause by visiting www.ScaresThatCare.org.